AF333720

I, MANCHA

by

Carol Spelius

cover artist: Ralph Harris

text illustrator: David Rau

layout editor: Wayne Spelius

guest editor: Susan Dunning

assistant editor: Michael Dunning

staff assistant: Ann Brashler

advisor: Christine Spelius

LAKE SHORE PUBLISHING
373 Ramsay Road
Deerfield, IL 60015

To all people who love animals.

To all Spanish-speaking people, young or old, who find themselves in a strange country with a new language and new customs.

To my grandchildren: Chris, Andrew, Michael, Ari, Heidi, Harley and Chiloe.

Special thanks to Ari for his support and confidence in I, MANCHA

Table of Contents

Chapter 1. My Beginnings. 1
Chapter 2. On the Streets. 7
Chapter 3. Prison Walls 13

Chapter 4. An Owner and a Home. 21
Chapter 5. Christina and School. 31
Chapter 6. The Stairs Versus Bladder 37

Chapter 7. My Friend, Rovero. 41
Chapter 8. Street Gangs. 45
Chapter 9. Heartbreak. 53

Chapter 10. Acapulco 57
Chapter 11. The Ocean & Sharks 63
Chapter 12. Mexico City Robber 69

Chapter 13. School Again and Raphael. 73
Chapter 14. Campus and a Car 77
Chapter 15. Chico 81

Chapter 16. Pregnancy & Puppies 85

Chapter 17. The Landlord & Chico 89

Chapter 18. Tragedy Strikes Again 93

Chapter 19. To the New World 95

Chapter 20. America. Idaho. 99

Chapter 21. Another Goodbye. 101

Chapter 22. Ranch Life Without Christina. 107

Chapter 23. School of Hard Knocks 113

Chapter 24. Return of Spring. 117

Chapter 1. My Beginnings

I, Mancha, was born in an empty orange-crate behind a store alley halfway between downtown Mexico City and the University. Yes, in an empty crate. Without a blanket to lie on. In the middle of the night. And it was raining.

To be born is such a trauma that those details did not bother me much, nor did the splinters in the wood or the fact that my brothers and sisters were still-born. Nature's instincts are so strong that even with my eyes closed, I found my mother's nipples, and that was enough comfort for me.

To this day, I can close my eyes and feel her rough tongue smoothing my coat, and her cool nose nudging me to eat. To this day, I love to be petted, and curled up beside a breathing body of some kind, man or beast. This may be a universal feeling, wanting to be loved.

I never knew my father, but he affected my life, anyway. From the looks of me, he must have been a Border Collie, or a shepherd breed of some kind -- maybe Australian. Whatever, he gave me brains, stamina and courage. Why else would I, a mere street dog, tackle telling my life's story? Even with some outside help, it has taken all the patience and insight I could muster. But I want to share with you, so, I continue my tale.

My mother, bless her soul, was a carefree bitch of careless breeding. She gave me my Mexican pride, my tough spirit, and a loving nature. She and I looked no more alike than black and white. She was short-haired, short-legged, and in the end, short- sighted.

We had some good times together, my mother and I, before I lost her. She would take me to play in *Chapultapec Park*, a place full of flowers and trees and picnicking families. And dogs. All kinds of dogs. Huge muzzled dogs on leashes, tiny hairless dogs not much bigger than sewer rats, and bushy-coated dogs with such long hair on their foreheads that their eyes were hidden. Most of the dogs belonged to families, but some were ownerless street-dogs like Mother and me.

Not belonging to anybody didn't matter so much to me, then, because I had my mother. She was an outrageous flirt and usually managed to beg food for us.

I was lucky my mother looked after me. I kept falling all over myself because of my big feet and long legs. I remember one time I tripped and sprawled on the grass in front of a mean kid. He grabbed me by the tail and squeezed my stomach until I couldn't catch my breath.

Mother barked at the baby's grandfather to get his attention. The grandfather rescued me just before my life was squeezed out. He also rewarded me with scraps of tortilla for not biting his grandchild.

I felt too sick to eat, but Mother relished every crumb. The grandfather held the baby's hand and taught him how to pet me gently. The lesson I learned was to keep my tail out of reach of anyone under three feet tall.

I figured Mother would always be there to look after me, so I was not prepared for that horrible day when she disappeared. We were on the sidewalk that runs beside Revolution Avenue. I was whining for Mother to give me lunch. Just then, a cat ran by. My flighty mother left me standing there with my mouth open while she chased after that infernal *gato*! They both dashed into the traffic in front of an *autobus* and were lost from view.

It was as if the traffic swallowed her. I know now, of course, what happened. The scene repeats itself every day in the city. The driver slams on his brakes, presses the horn, shouts a prayer. The big tires crush out life. The traffic is only slightly diverted, and the street-cleaner in his white coat sweeps up the remains.

I know now that living can't be taken for granted, but at that time, I stood at the sidewalk's edge, never dreaming that my mother wouldn't return. Finally I grew angry because I thought she had left me on purpose.

A shopkeeper who had heard the screeching of brakes and who may have guessed what had happened, offered me a saucer of milk and called me "poor little orphan."

The milk was not as warm and rich as Mother's, and I had difficulty managing the saucer, but hunger makes one learn quickly.

After I'd licked the dish clean, and licked up what I'd spilled, I wagged a thank-you and trotted back to the curb, dodging feet while waiting and waiting for my mother. I whined and carried on like a baby. Of course, she couldn't answer me.

My anger and hurt now changed to fear. What was going to happen to me if she didn't come back? Who would lick my face and cuddle me? The sidewalk seemed full of cruel, stamping feet. I cringed, huddling on the curb, afraid to move.

Later in the afternoon, my courage returned and I began to wander around seeking some trace of her. Twice I fell into sidewalk holes made from the last earthquake.

A fine mother I had, leaving her little pup alone like this. I'd bite her on the leg when I found her, I thought. But I didn't find her.

At last I came to *Chapultapec Park*. I hoped that she would be there, but of course she wasn't. There were so many children playing ball and screaming, and so many dogs running and barking, and so much confusion that I became even more frightened.

The world seemed too big for me. I willed my mother to come back to me. She didn't. I tried bargaining: All was forgiven. If she'd just come back, I'd never be cranky to her again. She didn't get that message, either.

Some nasty big boys began chasing me, and I squeezed through a wooden fence where they couldn't follow. Then some one yelled at me to get out of the flower bed.

I ran in another direction and caught a glimpse of a small dirty yellow dog. Floppy ears. Bowlegs. Bobbed tail. That had to be my mother. She was loping along in the distance, and I ran after her lickity cut until my lungs burned and my tongue hung out, dribbling.

When I finally caught up, I discovered I was chasing a vile-tempered male with a spiked collar. He bit my ear for my trouble and barked at me to get lost.

Lost? I already was lost, and so was my mother. Couldn't she hear me crying? Couldn't she see me, tail between my legs , wandering this big city all by myself?

As the sun dropped behind the volcanoes that rim the city, I happened back on to the big street where my mother had left me. The shops were all closed. I shivered with the evening chill that's caused by the mountain air settling into the valley. I felt very sorry for myself.

The doorway of my friend who had given me the milk was now barred with an iron grille. I cuddled up round and small, and as close to the warm bricks of the building as I could.

I didn't sleep well. When I awoke, I found myself crying. When I slept, I had nightmares of monsters stamping on Mother and me. That scared me awake. And so it went, all night long. Towards dawn, cold and miserable, I began to realize I might well be, as the shopkeeper had said, an orphan.

Chapter 2. On the Streets

When the sun came up, I, Mancha, faced the world alone. Luckily my wily mother had taught me how to sniff out mice in piles of rubbish, to defecate on the grass, never the sidewalk, and to be friendly to all, man or beast. I had lots more to learn.

The very first thing to learn was how to cross the streets safely. I waited for the flow of traffic to slow down, then I trotted out with purpose and direction, keeping a sharp eye and an alert ear, just in case. Believe me, horns blasting in your ears and the hot breath of cars ruffling your tail is a sure way to have fear nipping at your heels.

When I came to the very wide streets like *Revolution* and *Insurgentes*, I waited until traffic jammed to a halt, then I crossed with groups of people, stepping briskly to avoid being trampled. Even then, at one crossing, a heavy-footed *signora* clumped on my front paw, then fell over me, scattering her vegetables and a whole kilo of milk.

Santo Domingo! I yipped so loudly and jumped so high that three other people fell over themselves trying to avoid us. Another lesson for me: Keep head and tail as high as possible so I can see and be seen! And watch out for ladies who carry bundles or wear glasses.

I also learned to avoid those crossings where traffic comes at one in five directions. Cars sometimes honk and slow down, sometimes not. A lot of crashing and banging and swearing. I, Mancha, was not going to take any chances. Nor would I ever chase a cat. I did not want to disappear the way my mother did.

By the time I found the shop of my friend who had given me the milk the day before, I felt dizzy from the traffic fumes and all that exertion on an empty stomach.

"Aha, you came back," he shouted. (He's an old-time boot-maker, and quite deaf.) "I bet you want more milk!"

I wagged my tail, and he fed me again. He would adopt me if he could, he shouted, but his *senora* was sick with the asthma and allergic to dog-hair.

Lucky for me, I found out later. She often wielded the broom on her husband and friends, as well as dogs. She was even known to smash a full bottle of tequila on the brick floor of their shop when the money-box was found empty.

Meanwhile my days on the street passed. People went about their business without knowing or caring about my tragedy. I did the same to them.

Though I still grieved, I finally stopped looking for my missing mother, and I tried to stop being angry at her.

Nights were the hardest, when the shops closed and the sun went down. With no one to keep me warm, or to guard over me, I found it impossible not to cry. How lonely and forsaken I felt, and so sorry for myself. If I had known the truth, or been wiser, I might have grieved for my mother, whose life had been cut short.

I was not starving. I woke up every morning, alive. The restaurant owner next door to the boot-maker would toss me a few chicken feet after he'd boiled them for soup. In exchange, I listened to his stories of Mexican revolutions.

The baker on the same street was kindly also. He lived in his bakery and there, dogs are not allowed, so he'd come out on the sidewalk and teach me to sit up and beg for bits of bread that were too browned or had dropped on the floor.

These kind friends fed my heart as well as my stomach, and I was very careful not to wet on their floor, upset my milk, leave crumbs, or bark at their customers. If it hadn't been for them, I would have either starved or died of a broken heart.

As the weeks passed, the children who stood on the sidewalks selling Chiclets and Life Savers, became friendly, and just as it is for children with freckles or red hair, my description became my name. I was *Mancha* or "Spot" to everyone. I still belonged to no one, but I hid my sadness well.

Hunger was another matter. I actually drooled when I watched the street-venders slice off strips of meat for those lucky enough to have *pesos*. Sometimes a piece would drop to the ground. What a hustle. Sometimes I'd be the first dog to grab it, but never was I big enough to keep it. Sometimes a hungry child would beat us all. Then curses and boots kept even the most vicious dogs at bay until the child gulped the food whole or ran crying to his parents.

I was growing quite fast, I think, because I became braver, and stronger, and wandered further. One day, I passed many tall stone churches and many aroma-filled street-stands, until finally I reached *Zocalo*, the center of town where the city market is located. Tremendous crowds gather here. Dogs must be extremely careful not to get trampled, or worse.

My nose took me directly to the live animals. Some of the tourists complain about that stench, but I love those smells of chickens and ducks, even of the pigs and goats. Some were in cages, some were staked.

The best part of all was to see and smell the sheep. It sounds a bit *loco*, I must admit, but I,

Mancha, felt some kind of tie with those animals, some kind of longing to be with them.

I'd never seen sheep before, but they seemed to know me. Little did I know what would come to pass, and how important they would become to me.

I hung around their pens until almost dark, when a man with a club slung from his belt addressed me. "Little spotted dog, are you lost, or do you not have a home?"

Wagging my tail, I accepted his offer of a pat on the head and a few bits of chopped meat. I followed him, friendly as he was, and so sharing with his food. I hoped for a few more morsels before beginning my long trek back to my own neighborhood.

Can you imagine my surprise when he threw a net over my head? I jumped and squirmed trying to free myself. I only tangled myself more. I finally stood still, completely helpless, and too scared to bark. The man picked me up and threw me into the back of his truck, which was barred and screened to make a huge cage.

My loving and trusting mother had never
warned me against seemingly friendly people. For
sure, she had never tangled with a clever dog
catcher. And of course I didn't know who he was, or
why he was doing this to me.

There were lots of other dogs in the cage.
They weren't pleased, either. They barked so long
and hard that I got a headache. I promised myself
then and there that I would never bark unless my life
was in danger. I did allow myself to whine a little,
because I was so scared. I didn't know it then, but I,
Mancha, was on the way to the dog pound.

Chapter 3. Prison Walls

When we finally arrived at the dog pound, after a bumpy, noisy ride, all the dogs were sprayed and placed in another big cage. The keeper brought us some strange-looking food, strange-looking to me, because I, Mancha, had never eaten dry dog food. The others ate as if it were their last meal, but I wouldn't touch the stuff.

I didn't like the smell of the food. I didn't like the smell of the cage. I didn't like the smell of myself. I later learned that the awful smell was from the spray, and that it killed only germs, not dogs.

I now lay down in a corner, breathing as little as I could, and tried to sleep, willing myself to remember the good times when I had a mother, and when we had the park to play in. Then I thought of the shoemaker, who would miss my daily visits. And the restaurant owner with his tales of the revolutions, and the *tortillero* with his bits of *tortilla*. I knew they wouldn't miss me as much as I missed them. Some other friendly street dog could fill my place. That thought made me even sadder. I buried my head in my paws and whimpered, cry-baby that I was.

The cement floor was drafty, and of course smelly, but the part of me that hurt most was not my body, or my touchy nose, but my heart. To be misled by friendliness creates a wound that heals slowly. Finally, sleep rescued me, and I slept.

Morning came early, and I tried to stretch out all the aches and pains to the tune of the barking dogs and the shouting jailors. I realized another lesson I had learned. It is not true that misery loves company. I would have been most happy to be rid of all my cell-mates. They were so rude, and so ripe to fight. Twice, dogs knocked me down for no reason, and one who no doubt had a Great Dane for a grandfather, kept snarling at me, just asking for a battle. I ignored him, just as I did everybody else. The problem was, there was nowhere else to go. So I went inside myself. One can always remember, or imagine, or dream. It may not be reality, but it is survival.

About the third day of this prison camp, an even more dreadful clamor arose when a lady visitor came by. (We didn't have many.) Some of the dogs thought she could get them out of there, and the barking became chaotic. Even I found myself trying to climb the fence with the rest of them, vying for the visitor's attention. I didn't bark, but I whined, wagged my tail, flipped my ears up, pushed smaller dogs aside, and panted passionately. I was just as bad as the worst ones there. I was ashamed of my actions but I was part of the mob. That pack instinct we never lose.

I searched the face of the visitor, hoping to find some chord of empathy. Her hazel eyes stared back at me. Then she smiled. Completely forgetting the false face of the dog-catcher, I tried to lick her fingers that she held out to me. Was that not true love in her eyes?

She spoke some words to me in a foreign tongue and then walked on. I was devastated. Lady, please come back. I tried to jump out of the cage. Impossible even if I'd been the Great Dane.

Remembering the false friendship of the dog-catcher, and feeling duped again, I howled so loudly that I silenced some of the other dogs.

I sat down, sad and discouraged. I'd heard rumors. After so long, if one is not rescued by an owner, or bought on the spot, one is taken to the gas chamber. I didn't know then exactly what a gas chamber was, but it sounded as ominous as an *autobus.*

I learned later that sometimes the keeper held back a few of the healthier-looking dogs in hopes that the owners would come for them or that a visitor would buy them. Also, if one paid a bribe, the keeper would hold a dog for a few days to please a possible customer. This was not information to be bandied about and of course I, Mancha, had not heard about this, at that time.

Many days of misery passed. For a reason unknown to me, I was kept in the big pen. All my companions were taken away. The pen was suddenly very quiet and very lonely. I was sorry I had complained about the noise and crowds. Now I would have even welcomed the old snarling Dane.

One evening, as if some canine god was listening to my thoughts, another whole load of dogs from the streets was brought in. Spraying was repeated. Everything reeked again.

Most of these dogs looked as if they were owned by someone. Shampooed and manicured. Tags at their necks. Noses in the air. In the next few days I learned that the outside of a dog does not change the inside. These dogs were no different than the others. They were all scared and unhappy.

Being locked up was the worst, and then the mistrust one develops towards one's cell-mates. You wouldn't believe the fights. One Irish Setter was slashed so badly they removed him from the cage. I'm sure he bled to death.

Prisons are really cruel. I could not keep up my spirits. I thought I would never again be able to run around town, visiting shopkeepers or playing with children, or trusting anyone. I hid away in the corner. I snapped at any dog who came near me, even the big ones who could have beheaded me with one bite. I didn't care. I just wanted to be left alone to hate this awful prison world. I cried again for my mother.

The poundkeeper, who was a kindly man and who found it hard to face death each week for his charges, tried to cheer me. "Better days are ahead, little spotted doggie." I didn't believe him. I thought I'd rot in jail or be sent to the gas chamber.

The pound keeper proved to be right. In a few days, the visitor with the hazel eyes returned. All the dogs, even the elegant dogs who likely had owners, were going wild, barking and jumping and knocking each other over. All except me. In spite of the noise I heard her speak, in Spanish this time. "Yes. There she is, in the corner. The spotted one."

I lifted my head to look at her. I had no hope. I was dreaming her. She would dissappear again. She kept smiling and pointing at me. I wagged my tail, because of my friendly nature, and glanced behind me to see if someone else was there. No one was there. She must mean me. Had she come back for me? I lost all control. I wagged my whole body. No dream. My *amiga* had returned. Such happiness!

Then, even though the lady was smiling and nodding, the keeper looped a rope around my neck and pulled it tight. I thought he was going to strangle me. On the heels of such happiness, life seemed like a yo-yo. Up, down; up, down.

I braced my legs and resisted. He yanked the rope even tighter. I would have tried to bite him, or at least snarl, but my breath was leaving my body. My eyes were popping out of my head. I could not resist for long.

The keeper, my former friend, dragged me out of the cage. The door clanged shut and I thought my life was over. I lay trembling, ready for the end: an axe, the gas chamber, a rope choking me to death. The visitor knelt beside me and soothed me in that strange language that I know now as English. I could feel love in her hands, and with the return of air to my lungs, my spirit lifted. Maybe all was not lost, or was it just another up and down?

Standing up, she said to the keeper in Spanish, "Look at those spots. Her name has to be *Mancha*." I had recovered enough to wag my tail. Money changed hands, and the rope changed hands. Then I knew the visitor was for sure going to take me with her. I, Mancha, was finally to be free of the dog pound.

I tried to move so the rope wouldn't choke me, and at the same time examine my rescuer. This lady who had paid many *pesos* for my freedom was different than any Mexican I had met on the street. Her eyes were lighter brown and her skin was paler.

And *hijole!* To walk so fast in the heat of the day! Surely she was not *Mexicana.*

I broke into a trot to keep up with her, my new guardian. I felt much of the fear and sadness drain away from my heart, leaving space for love. To think, for the first time in my life, I belonged to some one. My mother would have been proud of me. I, Mancha, had an owner. This was to be my destiny.

Chapter 4. An Owner and a Home

"Christina!" A young man was standing by the open door of a small automobile, smiling at us. "A ride?"

I felt my hair rise as my new mistress climbed in and tried to pull me in with her. My experience with cars was limited. I connected my mother's disappearance with the *Autobus* and I would never forget how the ride in the dog-catcher's van led to the horrible time in the dog pound. I did not think that any good could come from an automobile.

I braced my legs and pulled back, thinking that this pale lady was not as big or as strong as the man at the dog pound. This lady, however, could have pulled my head right off my body. She stopped just short of that. Suddenly jumping out, she picked me up in her arms and climbed back in, holding me firmly on her lap.

"Rafael," she said, ". . . *me nueva perra grande, Mancha.*"

She thinks I'm a big dog, not a pup. I sat up as tall as I could. It felt good to have someone's arms around me and to have my back stroked. I stopped trembling as I began to watch the scenery whizz by with no effort on my part. I also found myself listening to my mistress and the driver talk Spanish. I had heard nothing but barking dogs, it seemed, for days on end, and the soft, melodic sounds were soothing to my ears.

Rafael seemed to drive well enough. Suddenly here we were, without an accident, on *Insurgentes Avenidos,* in a traffic jam. I decided it was fun to be in a car, watching people dodge and run around the stopped vehicles as Rafael honked his horn.

After some shouting, waving of arms, and beseeching help from above, Raphael was able to turn the car on to a quiet street called *Maria Velasco.* We stopped. I leaped out willingly, wagging my tail. I knew this street also. Raphael waved goodbye and drove off.

Christina walked me a few feet to an apartment building and unlocked the front door. I followed her in and the door clanged shut. My heart took a wild jump. What was this? Another jail? Had I been fooled again?

"Come on, Mancha. Up the stairs." I felt a gentle tugging. Stairs? Never. I could remember being barked at for starting down the stairs at the *Metro.* No. This was something I was certain my mother had warned me against. Christina kept tugging, but I, Mancha, kept pulling back. Everything seemed so unfriendly again, and I whimpered softly. Why was life this way?

All I wanted was a little corner where I could curl up to sleep, and a little milk once in a while, a friend or two, and a chance to walk around and see the world without causing any trouble, yet here my mistress was locking me up and urging me to do such a forbidden thing. I stared fearfully at the steps curling up to the sky. Never. Never. I shook my head, hoping the rope would release. I refused to lift my feet, slide as they would on the slippery marble.

"Mancha!" Her voice echoed up the empty stairwell as I braced against the rope once more.

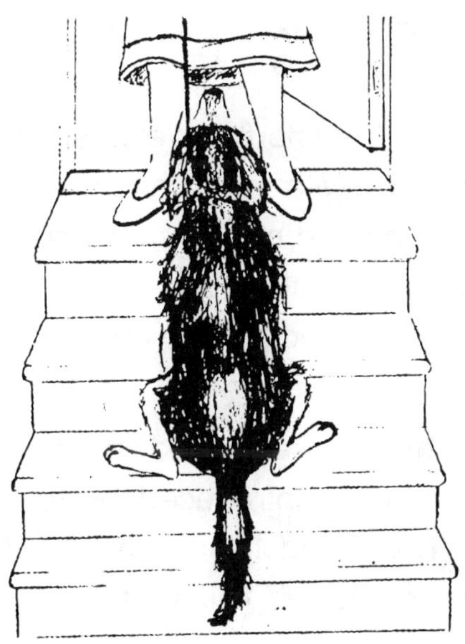

The pain shot through my neck, my eyes blurred, but nothing could make me climb those stairs.

Suddenly the pressure ceased. "All right, Mancha, I will carry you. This time." Christina pushed the strap of her leather bag over her shoulder, picked me up, and began to carry me up the stairs. Each flight was divided in half by a landing. On the second landing, someone peeked out her door to see what was happening.

"*Buenos Dias, Christina.* A dog?"

Christina said "Mrs. Gomez, this is Mancha."

Mrs. Gomez pointed a finger at me. "No bad dogs allowed here."

Christina set me down, and Mrs. Gomez came a little closer. "She seems like a nice dog." Mrs. Gomez patted my head gingerly. I tried to look grown up.

"*Si, Señora,* but heavy."

"Is she housebroken?"

"If she's not, she will be shortly or else she'll go back to the dog pound." With that, Christina picked me up again and carried me two more flights. Housebroken? I hoped she wouldn't break me. She seemed such a nice person. I licked her cheek. I had to trust her.

This time when Christina set me down, she took several deep breaths and introduced me to Mrs. Martinez and her two grandchildren, who also admired me and patted my head. This time I wagged my tail.

"Are you going to walk now?" Christina poked at me with the toe of her boot. I cringed and began to tremble. "Oh, Mancha, I'm not going to hurt you." Christina picked me up again. Three more flights.

Five altogether. Now panting by the time she arrived at her apartment, she put me down and unlocked her door.

"Mancha, if you don't learn to use the stairs, I'm going to have to take you back to the dog-pound." Christina said this in English. I, Mancha, did not know English at that time, so I wagged my tail and hung my head, only knowing that I was being scolded. Better than being broken.

After a bowl of milk and a tour of the apartment, I began to relax, even though my paws slipped and slid on the marble tile, and I kept bumping furniture when I wagged my tail. I had never been in a home before. I had never felt so clumsy.

Christina didn't seem to mind. She laughed and followed me around. "Mancha, this is the bathroom. This is the bedroom. That is my bed. And yes, you found the dirty clothes basket."

I liked best the roof-top patio or terrace of brick and concrete, off her living room. There were many large plants and a view of the mountains, the volcanos, the skyscrapers, the churches, and some smog below us, as well as a lot of people and traffic. There was also on the patio an open cage which was the home of her chicken whom I was not to chase.

In the room called the kitchen, Christina began to cook some food for us. The beef *sopa* made my mouth water, but I was mainly indifferent to the mango.

After eating, I became very nervous, but Christina solved that. She put the rope back around my neck and said "C'mon Mancha, I'll carry you downstairs and race you to the park."

That Christina can run as well as any dog. After I had attended to my duties, she took the rope off and we played with a ball until she began to pant. "I've got to save my strength so I can carry you back up those stairs." Afterwards, we both drank mightily in the kitchen.

"One more thing we have to do tonight." She led me into the bathroom. I looked at her to see if this was also a place to drink, but she pulled down a lid over the bowl. "You probably have never had a bath before, so you might not like it the first time."

What could I say? I watched the water pour into the big white tub with legs. So far so good. But when she lifted me up and stood me in the water, I began to whimper. She was right. I wasn't going to like this.

Christina ladled warm water on me until I was wetter than I'd ever been in any cloudburst. She now rubbed somthing smelly on me that she called shampoo. I must say it smelled better than the dog pound spray. She rubbed and scrubbed for a long time, talking to me all the while, then rinsed me off and wrapped me in a towel. Can you imagine that? I got free as fast as I could, and shook the water out of my coat the way any decent dog would.

"Wait a minute," Christina shouted, grabbing another towel, wrapping me again. "You're making a swamp out of the floor."

I was quite patient with her, I thought, but as soon as I was free again, I did the natural thing and shook 'til my teeth rattled. What dog can depend on a towel?

Still using a towel, Christina dried me some more and then brushed my coat. That brush made me a little nervous. I didn't know where it was going to land next or what it was going to do. It was obviously doing a fine job. I, Mancha, suddenly owned a beautiful, fluffy coat.

"Mancha, you look like an ad for shampoo."

Well, one is what one is, and if this small thing pleased her, so be it. I wagged to show my pleasure in her pleasure.

It had been a long, eventful day, but it was not quite over. "One more thing for you, Mancha," Christina said. "You'll get used to it." She knelt and held up, can you believe, a real leather collar, for me.

I held my head as high as I could and stood very still so she could place the collar around my neck. My very own collar, which really proved I had a mistress. An owner who cared for me.

Christina showed me where I could sleep, on a rug in the living room, but I was too excited to sleep with all these new smells, and my new smell, and my collar, and my mistress. I kept going into the bedroom to touch her face, just to make sure she was really there on the bed and that she was my friend.

Once she awakened out of a sound sleep with a jump because she was not used to having a wet nose stuck in her face. Her jump scared me so I dived under the bed, upsetting the alarm clock and a glass of water she'd set on the floor. She jumped up to mop up the water, and landed on my newly fluffed tail.

I yipped and cried and ran as far away as I could from this Christina who seemed suddenly to be my enemy, maybe another dog-catcher in disguise.

"Oh Mancha," she cried, running after me, scaring me even more. It is just a good thing that we had had our romp in the park or I might have had another accident and wet her floor again. I finally hid under the table in the kitchen. Christina got on her hands and knees and crawled under with me.

"Poor baby," she crooned in Spanish, soothing me. "An accident, Mancha. I'm so sorry." She petted me for some time, and I licked her hand in forgiveness. "You were lucky I didn't have shoes on," she said.

We both crawled out from under the table, and Christina heated some milk, pouring a bowl for each of us. She then put a sweater on the floor beside her bed for me to lie on. How nice to be surrounded by my newly found mistress's odor. Much better than a strange rug. Or a corner of an alley. Or the dog pound. By the time we finally settled down to sleep, I knew that Christina and I were truly friends, *Amigas* forever.

Yes, it had been a remarkable day for me. I would try to forget the bad things and remember

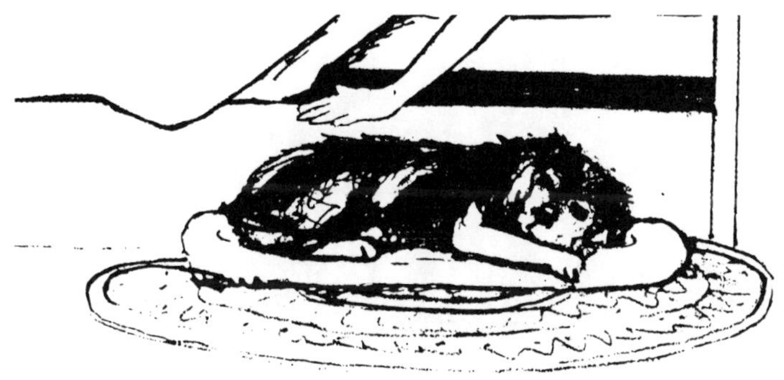

only that if I lifted my head slightly, there was my friend Christina's hand, hanging from the bed. It was almost as warm a feeling as having my mother back again. Feeling the touch of my soft leather collar around my neck, I, Mancha, fell asleep without worrying at all about what the future would bring.

Chapter 5. Christina and School

I've found that if one hasn't known hardship, one can't value luxury. To awaken without a boot from behind or a yell in your ear, is a treat. To awaken dry and warm and next to a friend when you have experienced otherwise, is close to what I think might be Heaven.

I stretched and wiggled. Christina yawned her good morning and asked "Want to go to school with me?" She said she had a surprise for me. The tone of her voice sounded good to me.

At that time, I, Mancha, had never been to school, didn't really know what school was, but I knew the word "go." I was wagging with excitement, but just outside the door, I stopped abruptly. The stairwell had not gone away. All my fears came back. I began to whimper and tremble.

"Oh, Mancha, you're a pain!" Christina said. "You will have to get over this." But she picked me up and carried me down the five flights of stairs again. Going down was much easier for her than going up.

After Christina unlocked the front door, I dashed to a nearby plot of grass and Christina hailed a taxi. She expained to me that dogs are not

allowed on the *Auto-buses* or the *Metro* which is the
subway, and since the *Universitaria* was too far
away to walk to, and since she had no friends who
were driving that morning, and since hitch-hiking is
not the custom in Mexico, the taxi was the only way
to go.

I found the taxi-driver not nearly as smooth a
driver as Raphael. He wheeled in and out of lanes,
drove far too fast, then slammed his brakes on. I slid
off the seat six times in fifteen minutes, and finally
Christina held me in her lap. Such a relief to get out
of that taxi. I don't like them. Too dangerous in or
out!

Christina paid the *pesos* and said at least a
taxi was a lot cheaper here than in Chicago. It did
get us to the *Universitaria.*

The University of Mexico is an impressive
place to a dog, and I would imagine, to anyone.
Huge colorful buildings surrounded by palm trees
and pepper trees and grass and flowers and more
people than you'd find at any market.

I, Mancha, stayed very close to Christina so we
wouldn't lose each other. Lucky for me, because as
we turned a corner we came to a gathering of
dozens of dogs and owners, all barking and
shouting. If this was the surprise, I didn't like it.

All that barking reminded me of the dog pound,
but Christina knelt to soothe me, and shortened the

leash which she had hooked to my new collar. "A couple of veterinarian classes have grouped together for a dog judging," she said. I looked into her face, carefully. This was obviously not the surprise, either.

"We are going to the laboratory," she said. With that, we both trotted past all that noise and confusion of a hundred dogs and came to the doctor's office.

I didn't like the real surprise too much. I watched Christina dress in a white lab coat and prepare a needle for the doctor. Then she held me firmly, which was all right. She said "Be a good doggy and don't growl." The doctor said "This won't hurt." Then he stabbed me.

"It's just a rabies shot," Christina said, "And the next one I'll give to you, myself."

In spite of the indignity of the needle, the day on campus I enjoyed very much. We had lunch under a pepper tree and Christina introduced me to some of her classmates. One was a pale blond *Americano* and one a very dark *Africano*. I was also very happy to again see Raphael, who greeted me warmly.

Raphael said "Christina, I have a present for you, if Mancha approves." Why would he say such a thing as that? We found out shortly when we walked over to the parking lot with him. He opened the car door and brought out a basket. In the basket was a small ball of black fur that sneezed, opened its eyes and mewed.

A kitten is not so far from a cat, and the word *gato* does not charm me. In fact it brings to mind the sad ending of my mother, and something else. Jealousy. I did not wish to share my new home with a cat.

I looked coldly at the contents of that basket. A growl rose in my throat but stopped midway. I swear that little kitten smiled at me. He looked right at me with his dark blue eyes and smiled. Then yawned. Then tried to climb out of the basket.

"He's not a bit afraid of you, Mancha," Christina said. And why should he be? If I knew enough not to chase a chicken, I could put up with a kitten, as long as he didn't turn himself into a cat. I put my nose up to his nose and wagged my tail.

Raphael said "I guess they'll get along," and offered to drive us home. Christina held the basket in her lap but she kept an arm around me so I wouldn't feel jealous. She needn't have bothered because I felt jealous anyway.

At the apartment, we set up the kitty's litter box on the patio beside the chicken cage. Raphael said Christina should live in the country, and Christina said she intended to, and Raphael asked "In Mexico with me, Christina?" and Christina looked sad and said "No, Raphael, in the States." Then it was Raphael's turn to look sad. He probably was jealous, also. I licked his hand in sympathy.

That night the kitten, whom Christina named *Negrito* because of his black color, crawled off Christina's bed and joined me on the floor. I gave him a very quiet warning growl, because I didn't want to disturb Christina. He was so busy purring that he didn't notice. He cuddled up close to me and purred away, his little eyes like green lights. Finally, he fell asleep. Then I was so afraid of rolling on him, I couldn't sleep. I lay there in the dark for a long time, afraid to move.

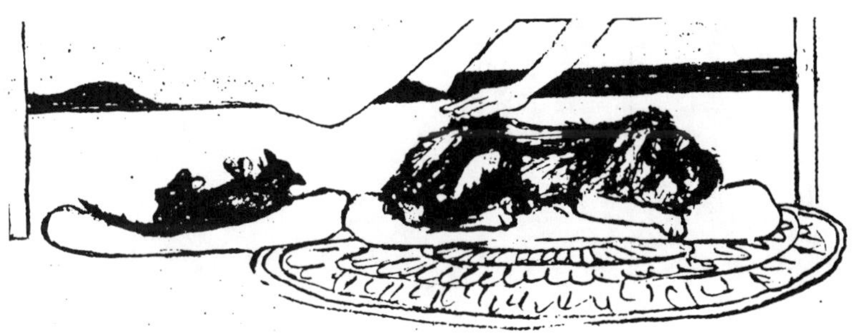

Chapter 6. The Stairs Versus Bladder

The next week passed quickly. Raphael came over often to see the kitten, and he joined Christina and me in the park for our evening play. He thought Christina was spoiling me by carrying me up and down the stairs, but when he saw how scared I was, he carried me, himself, when he was there.

Raphael and Christina sat at the kitchen table for hours at a time with various other students, reading and talking and laughing.

I, Mancha, always kept one eye on Christina to make sure she was not being molested. If anyone got too close to her I would get up and growl. A protective instinct inherited from my father, I guess. I felt the same about the kitten and the chicken, and later, our goat, but always the most about Christina. Those students laughed at me, but I was serious. If they had hurt her I would have torn them apart.

As more weeks passed, I, though half grown, and so brave in many ways, still feared the stairway. Twice a day Christina packed me up and down the five flights.

I was ashamed of myself. When Christina and I would go for a walk and we'd run into some of my old friends, they would tell her what a great dog I was, and admire my fluffy coat and new muscle. "Mancha so brave, *Senorita*." If they only knew what a coward I was on the stairs.

Christina complained to Raphael when he came to see us. "Mancha's getting heavier every day, and I've lost ten pounds, packing her up and down."

Raphael smiled, shrugged, raised his eyebrows and said something like "*Aventa*," which translates into English something like "Relax, take it easy, don't fight the revolution by yourself, tomorrow will be better . . . "

And so it came to pass. One day Christina was late getting back home from the University. Very late. She had waited for a less crowded bus because she was afraid to hang onto the outside of an *autobus* the way many Mexican students do.

By the time Christina arrived home, I was very restless and eager to get outside. In fact, my fear of wetting the marble floors was greater than my fear of the stairs.

When Christina opened the door to the apartment, I bounded past her and raced down the five flights of stairs without a thought of danger. Christina raced down right behind me, carrying the key to the street door. All turned out well, and from then on, I, Mancha was not afraid of stairways, either up or down, and you can believe my mistress was very pleased with that!

She laughingly called me "house-broken", which I translated as breaking out of the house, because from this point on, I didn't stay at home with the chicken and the kitten so much, even though they missed me. I followed Christina wherever she went except on the *autobus* or the *Metro* which is the subway, and not very often to the great University, of course, because taxis weren't that cheap.

In the mornings, when we heard the bell or saw the bellman walking down the center of the street heralding the garbage truck's coming, Christina carried the garbage bag down and I accompanied her. Then we would run around the block together, before breakfast.

It was a happiness for me, Mancha, to be able to visit again all the fascinating places in the neighborhood, to come home whenever I pleased to a roof over my head, and to friends, and best of all, to have an owner. Even though Christina was not *macho*, and not even *Mexicano,* I was very proud of her.

I accompanied her to *el banco* on the corner and waited outside while she exchanged a check for *pesos*, and then to the big super-market across *Insurgentes Avenido*, where again I waited outside

while she bought groceries to be carried in plastic
bags which she used later for garbage. And it was
on one of those trips when I, Mancha, met *Rovero*.

40

Chapter 7. My Friend, Rovero

Chickens are O.K. and kittens are very amusing, but I think besides one's owner, whom you love more than life itself, the best possible friend for a dog is another dog.

Rovero and I were *simpatico.* We spoke the same language, as it were.

It seems such a coincidence that I, Mancha, was waiting for my mistress outside the market, at the same time that Rovero was waiting for his mistress. We sniffed at each other warily at first and then we both knew we would be *amigos.* Later, when I matured, he became my mate.

Rovero did not have that skinny look of a street dog. Not that it would have made any difference. It was his spirit that I loved. His solid black coat was short and shiny, and I was fascinated with his webbed feet. I knew ducks had webbed feet, but dogs?

Nor was Rovero a country dog, in with the farmers for the *Mercado*, a dog that I might not see again. Rovero was an apartment dog. An apartment *perro* who lived only one block away and who went for walks with his mistress every day.

There are some dogs in Mexico City who are never let out, not even on a leash. They spend their entire lives in a small yard or on a roof top. Barking seems to be their only form of amusement. Rovero and I were lucky, not to be kept like prisoners, and to be able to find each other.

Christina assured Rovero's owner that he was in safe company when he was out with me. I don't know how true that was. Rovero wasn't as streetwise as I, and didn't know as many places to go and people to see, but I, Mancha, changed all that.

Each day, when his owner let him out, Rovero came to the door of my apartment house and waited on the sidewalk until I appeared, if I were not already out and waiting at his apartment house.

Each school day, we escorted Christina to the street where she boarded an *autobus* to the University. She never more worried about my being lonely because I had Rovero to play with. Sometimes I felt a little guilty neglecting Negrito during the day, but then Negrito could always talk to the chicken.

After saying goodbye to Christina, or rather Christina saying goodbye to us, we'd trot off together to find the busiest streets where we could see the street peddlers and the beggars and the *touristas.*

I'll never forget the first time I took Rovero to the flower mart. Good Heavens! He didn't know too much. It was all right for us to sniff at the roses in the clay vases and the gardenias in the buckets, but Rovero lifted his leg on a bushel basket of carnations. At the sight of this act, the owner turned into a volcano, throwing pebbles and words at us. "You craven offspring of knot-headed devils. Out! Out! Never come here again, you clumsy savages."

We both ran. How could we explain or apologize? On our getaway, sad to say, we tromped on a sidewalk display of grains, vegetables and jewelry, scattering everything as we ran. One merchant threw a bucket of slop at us, and another whacked mightily with a stout stick on Rovero's shoulder. Rovero yipped for two blocks and limped for a week. In our travels henceforth, we always bypassed that particular street. However, that did not keep trouble from following us.

Chapter 8. Street Gangs

Rovero and I were off playing in one of my favorite vacant lots where there are always plenty of rats to chase in amongst the trash. Suddenly a pack of street dogs surrounded us. There was not time or space to run away.

These dogs were some of the toughest mongrels in Mexico City. I had seen them before but had always been able to keep my distance.

The ringleader, an obvious veteran of many battles, was nicknamed "The General" by no less than the police chief of Mexico City. He looked like a cross between a Boxer and a Pit Bull. He stood directly in front of Rovero, cutting off any escape.

Rovero had never in his whole life battled another dog. Remember, Rovero was not a street dog. He not only had always lived in a home, but he had a fine pure pedigree and papers to prove it. None of this prepared him for a street fight.

He might have tried tucking his tail between his legs and slinking away. He might have gotten away with that, but the thought never crossed his mind. Rovero stood, friendly and polite, head up, ears forward, not recognizing danger at all.

It was one of those loaded moments forever held in my memory. No sound. No movement. "The General," whose expertise had come from tough, life-threatening street-fighting experience, broke the spell. He growled, and the hair stood up on the back of my neck. Drool dripped from his long yellowed teeth as he lunged toward's Rovero's jugular vein. I thought it was all over for Rovero.

There was a flurry of dust and barking and bodies flying. I threw myself into the battle, nipping the heels of the General, hoping he would let go of my friend's throat.

My teeth, sharp enough, bounced off scar tissue. Bloodless. Nerveless. " The General" paid no more attention to me than to a lap dog. I was not going to save my friend's life by those tactics. Great mother of mercy! Help was what we needed.

I leaped over the snarling bodies and sped around the corner to the shoemaker's. Barking in a frenzy, I managed to get his attention.

"I hear you, Mancha, my friend. What in God's name do you want?" He followed me in his ambling gait back to the battlefield.

The General held Rovero by the throat and was shaking him from side to side, blood splattering like red rain. The shoemaker carried a whistle on a chain around his neck and he blew it as hard as he could. The street dogs, probably thinking it was the

46

police, or worse, the dogcatcher, brought themselves up short and vanished without a bark.

Rovero lay limp in the dirt, blood oozing from his neck. The shoemaker rushed back to his shop and brought a pan of water. First he offered Rovero a drink. Rovero could not lift his head. The shoemaker, after pouring a bit on Rovero's tongue, tried to bathe the wound with what was left.

Just then, the shoemaker's wife came like a truck around the corner, her broom in her hand. "A customer is waiting!" she yelled. "Why do you leave the shop when a customer wants his shoes? Are you *loco*?"

The shoemaker looked from me to his wife to Rovero. The shoemaker decided against any more violence taking place. "I'll come back as soon as I can, Mancha, to help your friend." I wagged my thanks as he meekly followed his irate wife back to his untended shop.

Rovero's broad leather collar was in tatters, but it had helped save his life. I looked at him closely. *Dios!* What was I to do. I was no doctor but I sensed that if I waited for my shoemaker friend to come back, Rovero might bleed to death.

I ran back and barked at Rovero's apartment, but no one was home. I knew the chicken or the kitten would be no help. Christina was at the University, too far away for me to fetch. I returned to

Rovero, but he had his eyes closed. The blood was still running from his neck. I hoped that meant his heart was still beating.

I had to think of something! If I stopped a stranger on the street in my excited condition, they'd think me mad and yell for help, themselves. Dear God, what to do? The thought came to me: The clinic! The veterinary clinic in this neighborhood. Six blocks away, and with only one bad crossing. Why hadn't I thought of that sooner? Christina and some of the other veterinary students worked there, part time.

Dodging people and cars, I loped like a horse, all the way. But of course they keep the clinic door closed. I barked and barked but no one came. I was hoping some one would call the police for me disturbing the peace. Finally a customer, carrying her Mexican hairless dog, opened the door to enter. I bounded in ahead of her, bumping her knees and almost knocking her down. She spewed out some street words I didn't expect a lady to know. I was lucky she didn't kick me.

Raphael was on duty. I wheedled and whined at him, pulling his pant leg, and beseeching him with my eyes to come with me. The doctor himself came out of his office at the commotion. "Isn't that Christina's dog?"

"*Si*," Raphael said, "but she's acting crazy."

"She obviously wants you to go with her. Why don't you see what it's all about?" The doctor knelt and petted me. "She's not frothing at the mouth. Go with her. Christina can make up your time." I kissed the doctor and wagged and turned myself practically inside out, then tugged at Raphael's pant leg, and raced toward the door. Come on, Raphael!

Raphael is no fast runner like Christina. He smokes too many cigarettes. I got very impatient with him, but we made it in time. Rovero was unconscious but still breathing. I could see his ribs rise and fall. Thank the saints!

Raphael is not a big man, but he is strong. He quickly took off his white jacket and placed it beside Rovero. He then stuffed his handkerchief in the biggest wound on Rovero's neck, rolled Rovero onto the jacket, and picked him up, jacket and all. I kept dashing ahead and then racing back.

" I can't run with him, Mancha, so relax." How could I relax? I ran ahead, then retraced my steps, ran on ahead, and repeated myself. Again and again. We finally got to the clinic. *Caramba!* I was as winded as Raphael.

The doctor put Rovero to sleep, even though he was already unconscious, and sewed him up. Rovero remained there, for days, a very sick dog. Many times the doctor allowed me to sit beside

Rovero's cage, which smelled somewhat like the dog pound.

Rovero had a sore neck for quite awhile, and many nicks and scratches in his shiny black coat. He also gained in alertness to all danger, not just automobiles.

Never again did Rovero allow any dog to come within speaking distance without having to give credentials. He became a fighter, hostile to strangers, for which I was sorry, since I am basically a pacifist unless my home and family are threatened.

Now, during our around-town travels, Rovero managed to single out and fight every one of those dogs from that pack and make them run off howling. Except for "the General," who never seemed to travel alone. Rovero was not stupid, and I was grateful for that. I don't think Rovero, even as strong as he was, could have survived the General twice, with or without his cronies.

Those were our days of adolescent escapades. I had no special goal in life. I did, however, take seriously my responsibilities to Christina. Rovero would accompany me in the late afternoon to meet every bus so that when Christina arrived, we could walk her home.

I had never been so happy. My own home, a loving mistress, and a loving friend to share my days, not to mention a fresh egg every once in a while, and an attentive kitten to play with during the evening. What more could a dog ask for? *Dios Mio!* I, Mancha, was tempting fate.

Chapter 9. Heartbreak

And then it happened. One day, Rovero did not come to our door. I went down to his apartment and waited at his gate, but no Rovero. This was not like my friend to be elsewhere. I couldn't help thinking it was exactly how my mother left me. Without a word. I whined a little and waited some more. I went on my rounds of visiting the shopkeepers and came back and waited. No Rovero.

Maybe, like my mother, Rovero had also been killed by an *autobus*. The thought was so sickening I couldn't look at a street cleaner without growling. Had he brushed up the remains of my dear friend and tossed them in his trash can?

Everything in my life came to a standstill. I waited at Rovero's gate hour after hour, day after day.

Christina missed Rovero, too. After a week of no Rovero, and seeing one unhappy Mancha, Christina went down to Rovero's apartment house with me and rang the buzzer.

A lady who was not Rovero's mistress, greeted us. *"Buenos noches, Senorita."* No, they did not own a dog. They had just moved in. No, she did not know where the other people had moved to. My Rovero was gone. Gone for good.

It is hard to believe that life can be so hard at times, but it is. I lost interest in the streets. I quit watching the people pass by. I got tired of watching my friend Pedro squeeze orange juice at his sidewalk stand in front of the bank. I quit visiting my old friends the baker and the shoemaker.

Mrs. Rodrigez on the 4th floor gave me a beautiful marrow bone, and Mrs. Gomez on the 2nd landing bought a whole box of dog biscuits for me and said "*Pobrecita*, we want you to be happy here." Nothing helped. I was sick with loss.

When Christina left for class, I cried and cried, wanting her to stay with me but not wanting to accompany her to the *autobus*. I moped on the patio with Negrito and the chicken. Negrito tried to amuse me with his clever antics, playing with string and attacking a ball. The chicken kept walking all over me, trying to gain my attention, but all I could do was hide my head in my paws and sigh a lot.

When Christina came home, I followed her around like a shadow, causing Christina to trip a number of times and lose her temper. "Mancha, you are making me nervous!" she cried. I, Mancha, was nervous, too. I was afraid that my mistress would disappear also and then I would be alone again in the world, without anyone to love, or to love me. I wasn't going to let that happen if I could help it. So I continued to make Christina nervous, hovering close to her at all times.

I began having nightmares of Negrito falling off the patio five floors down on to *Maria Velasco,* that busy street; of Christina being kidnapped, and of the chicken being stolen and eaten. My sadness made me cranky with Christina's friends, even Raphael. I growled and barked at him when he tried to hug Christina.

The night the four students came over to study for a test, I wouldn't allow them to enter our apartment, so Christina locked me in the bedroom. I still kept growling occasionally.

One evening after a particularly trying day, Christina said "Mancha, what we both need is an outing." Four buses had passed her by, her early morning class had been canceled but there had been no announcement ahead of time, and she'd flunked a test on naming the states and capitols of all of Mexico. "There's a vacation coming. Maybe we can spend some time in the country."

Mrs. Gomez volunteered to care for the kitten and the chicken, but that was only the first step to an outing, I found out. Christina had no car, and no money for an airplane ticket. Dogs are not allowed on the *autobus.* That left us very few choices, but in the end, it worked out.

Jose, another veterinary student, was driving to
Acapulco, where his parents lived on a mountain
near the sea, and he invited us both to come home
with him. His sister Amelita and his brother Juan
were also coming, and two of their friends. I,
Mancha, was the only dog invited.

I tried to act happy for Christina's sake, but she
knew how I felt. "Mancha, I promise you, no one
dies of a broken heart. You'll see." I hoped she was
right.

Chapter 10. Acapulco

Cars in Mexico are usually small, and there were seven of us. I, Mancha, sat on Christina's feet most of the way, wishing we had never come. Jose was a nice enough sort and always spoke kindly to me, but he was a very fast driver. The dents in his fenders did not speak well of his driving skills, either.

I couldn't help thinking how sad it would be after surviving city traffic and taxis, to be toppled off a mountain top with no one at fault but the driver of the car one was in. And such terrible curves. I felt that Jose put far too much faith in his religious saints, especially when the car had such poor brakes and worn-out tires. I felt dizzy and sick.

Jose pulled off the highway and stopped for me and Christina to run. We cut through a mountain meadow and suddenly came upon a bunch of sheep tended by a young boy. The sheep were eating the grass, and the growth was so heavy they hardly moved, just stood there chewing and chewing, turning their little pointed noses so they could watch us.

I could tell they wanted to play. I jumped in amongst them and barked a greeting. Suddenly the lambs and the sheep were running every which way and Christina was yelling at me to stop and the herder was yelling and chasing the sheep.

I, Mancha, felt that same familiar warmth towards those sheep that I had at the *Zocalo* in Mexico City, but nobody else seemed to understand how I felt. Christina grabbed my collar and snapped my leash on and apologized to the herder who was just a young boy. He had lost his straw hat in the race to gather up his flock, and had cut his bare foot on a rock.

Christina had the proper things in her shoulder bag to treat the injury: a bottle of spray stuff and a band-aid. The herder held my leash and petted me while Christina doctored his foot. She also found his hat for him. "Mancha has never before been out of Mexico City. She doesn't know how to act around farm animals."

I hung my head, wishing to disappear like a rabbit down a hole.

"She could learn," the boy said, not wanting to hand me back. I wagged my tail. Of course I could learn.

"Would you sell her to me for ten *pesos?*"

I, Mancha, stood up taller. Ten *pesos!*

"Not for a hundred," Christina said, "even though what Mancha knows about sheep is not worth two *pesos.*"

"She could learn," the young boy said again, handing back the leash.

"I'm sure she could," Christina said, holding me fast. "Maybe some day she will."

I really wished we could stay with the sheep all day in that beautiful meadow rimmed with mountain tops and forests, and forget about Acapulco, and the dangerous curves, and that most uncomfortable car, but of course I couldn't explain all that to Christina. I reluctantly followed her back to the road, knowing that in a short time I would be feeling dizzy and sick again.

"Mancha," she said, "I suppose I'm cruel to keep you in a big city when you enjoy the country." She looked so sad, I licked her hand. Didn't she know that she was the important thing? Not fresh air, space, sheep, or food. I would stay with her above all else, even above Rovero if he should appear like a vision, right now.

Ah, my Rovero. The thought of him made me sad again. Was he missing me, also?

We all climbed back in the car and it seemed more crowded than ever. "Move, Mancha, you're sitting on my foot," complained Amelita. I shifted to Christina's.

We finally arrived in Acapulco safely, with only two of us getting carsick. (Better that, than getting killed.)

Jose's parents welcomed all the guests, including me, making us feel welcome. Their house had no glass or screens on the windows and the door was seldom closed. The house had one big room where the cooking and visiting and the sleeping were done. It was a crowded but happy place with nine children, and three cats whom I ignored.

I found Acapulco too warm for my taste, or I should say, for my heavy coat. Everyone spent more time outside than in. Even so, I panted all the time from the heat.

Jose's parents raised chickens and pigs so they had plenty to eat. They also had a mango tree, a fig tree, and a papaya tree. The grandmother baked bread in a stone oven, outside.

Christina and I went out to watch Jose milk the goat tethered behind the house. It was just after the rainy season so the grass was lush and nourishing and the milk, rich. Jose squirted the milk right into the cats' mouths, but I felt too shy to line up for that, so I pretended I hadn't noticed.

Christina and I ran all over the mountain trails until she was panting also. Then we sat beside Jose and the others for a long time in the moonlight.

When everyone went to bed, the students lying on their bedding made a solid carpet of bodies and I had to step carefully to reach Christina in the dark. I had already searched the place for scorpions, but one couldn't be too sure of what could come through the open doors and windows during the night.

I kept looking for danger. I licked Christina's face occasionally so she'd know I was there, got scolded by Amelita for stepping on her, and got kicked by Jose's friend for waking him. Meanwhile, for the first time all day, I had time to miss Rovero.

I pretended he was there beside me, guarding Christina. I pretended that we'd see him on the street, tomorrow. I knew better. He was gone forever. I checked on Christina again. "Mancha!" she hissed. "Quit waking me up!"

Chapter 11. The Ocean & Sharks

The next day everyone, including the grandmother, went swimming in Acapulco Bay. I understood the swimming. The thing I couldn't understand was how grown people could spend hours lying on the sand in that hot Acapulco sunshine, frying themselves with oil.

I finally deserted them and found some shade near a terrace where I could keep an eye on Christina but be comfortable. The sun was making Christina look more and more like a *Mexicana* so some good might come of it.

After a time, Christina headed back to the water again. She began to swim quite a ways out with Emalita and I became very disturbed. I like puddles to play in. I even don't mind a tub of water for a bath. A pond is also fun. But an ocean? That is too much water.

I seldom bark, but I wanted Christina to get out of that water. Who knows what's in there besides people? I felt an unbearable unease. I waded in and barked and barked until my throat hurt, but she couldn't hear me, even though I startled plenty of other swimmers and got them out of the water. It seemed that I would have to go on in after Christina, deep water and all.

I am not the greatest swimmer in the world, but I swam out as fast as I could, with my poky dog paddle. Fear did not improve my swimming skills. I thought Christina would never turn around and see me. There were some good-size waves and I was beginning to think that I might drown, when Christina finally stopped and turned around.

"Mancha, what are you doing out here?" I tried to reply, but got my mouth full of water.

Emalita and Christina swam on either side of me, urging me back to shore. I needed no urging as long as they were coming with me. I wanted us to get out of that ocean.

"You are way too far out, Mancha," Christina said, between strokes. All of us are, I thought, and swam as fast as I could.

We were still wading in, Christina still chiding me, and me scarcely able to lift my head from exhaustion, when we heard the first screams of "Shark! *Animalitos! Mio Dios!* Out! Out!"

I knew it. Something had told me. Smell, vibrations, special sense. Something had warned me. I wanted to jump all over Christina with joy that I'd gotten her out of the water, but all I could manage was a weak tail-wag and a lick on the cheek.

There was a mass exodus from the water, with screams and splashes filling the air, and people pointing to a black fin coming in closer to shore.

"The dog was right!" people kept saying. "Not a good day to be in when sharks are around."

Nobody went back into the water that day. Emalita said that I, Mancha, had saved their lives. Other people, including those that hadn't liked my barking and had said I shouldn't be at the beach, came and thanked me, also.

I did feel proud. After I regained my strength, I pranced around with my head held high, and kept nudging Christina so she wouldn't forget me.

About half the student body of the University of Mexico seemed to be strolling the beach, excited about the sharks. I even spied Raphael a few hundred yards away and dashed down to greet him. After all, Raphael was Christina's dearest friend. But Raphael looked startled and embarrassed.

Christina looked at Raphael and at the young woman hanging on to Raphael. I do not think Christina was so pleased to see the young woman draping herself onto Raphael, but she didn't say.

Everything about that woman seemed nervous. Beautiful, but nervous. Her shiny hair swished, her long legs wriggled, and her black eyelashes fluttered. She was making *me* nervous. Was she afraid of Christina? Or of Raphael? I couldn't tell. She patted my head. She didn't seem afraid of me.

Raphael looked at Christina and then looked at Jose and his eight brothers and sisters. Raphael looked angry. He did not smile. I kept wagging my tail and nudging, to make him feel better. He seemed to ignore me.

"Hello, Teressa. Hello Raphael," Christina said, and she smiled at them. She did not simply bare her teeth. She really smiled. And what I thought might have been an awkward moment turned into a smiling, happy time. After all it was a vacation, exams were done, and no one had been eaten by a shark.

A time to celebrate, even without Rovero. I had discovered that you can bury grief like you bury a bone. You know it's there but you are not gnawing on it all the time. You'll get to it later.

I must say Raphael did not talk much, or smile much. I did touch his hand several times but he did not touch back.

That evening there was dancing under the stars, and a fish barbecue, and everyone sang Mexican folk songs, and my Christina was having such a good time I thought my heart might break with happiness for her. And I, Mancha, had saved Christina and her friends from the sharks. If I had been a cat, I would have purred.

Chapter 12. Mexico City Robber

Our trip back to Mexico City was uneventful. I slept all the way. We walked up the flights of stairs quietly, tired and glowing from the day on the beach, and carrying more than a little Acapulco sand between our toes. We were glad to be home again, which proves it was a worthy outing.

As Christina unlocked the door to our apartment, I heard a faint scuffling noise, and as the door swung open, we surprised a man standing in the middle of the living room. He was a robber. He had our radio in his hand.

Frantic for the safety of my mistress and our home, I bounded in. The robber dived through the opened door to the patio, letting the radio fall to the floor.

I followed him as fast and as noisily as I could. He jumped and grabbed the top of the brick wall that divides us from the laundry area just as I jumped up and grabbed him by the seat of the pants. The denim ripped and I got a kick in the chin as he scrambled over the top of the wall and out of sight.

By the time Christina and I came back through the patio door and through the living room and around to the laundry area, we saw the robber going over another wall and onto the roof of the building next door. *Dios!*

We went back and searched the apartment for an accomplice. Christina checked the radio. It still worked. She took inventory: camera, binoculars, books. Nothing was missing. We must have come home shortly after he had entered the apartment. I could tell Christina was thinking the same thing I was. Would he come back?

The next day, workmen were busy putting bars on the windows and a double-bolted lock on both doors. Mrs. Rodrigez came to look and so did Mrs. Gomez. We were all so relieved. The robber could have taken the chicken!

Robbers are so common in Mexico City that even the laundry is hung in locked cages to dry on the roof tops. Maybe we were lucky not to have had a robber in our apartment before this.

We all felt happy when the workmen were done and gone. "Mancha, you didn't even trust the locksmith!" Chistina said. She was right. I think that the locksmith tried to steal an egg from the chicken.

My new motto was bark first and look afterward if anyone came across our threshold without an invitation. I didn't realize it then, but I was becoming almost as mean and tough as poor Rovero had become after his fight with the General.

Chapter 13. School Again and Raphael

It is always exciting, that first day back to school. Of course for me at that time, it was back to the bus-stop. Late afternoon, I, Mancha, began to hang around the corner, waiting for Christina to get off the *autobus.*

I soon noticed someone else hanging around: our good friend Raphael. He was alone, without his Acapulco *tamale.* He had parked his car which was really his brother's with whom he stays in Mexico City. He carried his books in his back-pack and a bouquet of flowers in his hand.

He was much friendlier than he had been on the beach. Oh, yes. He patted me and we both squatted down close to a building out of the way of people's feet.

After sitting quietly for a long time stroking my neck, while three loaded buses went by without Christina, Raphael asked, "Mancha, are you ever jealous?"

I studied his somber eyes and wagged my tail. I, Mancha, knew what he was talking about. Sometimes I did not like even Raphael to be around Christina.

I remembered the time Christina baby-sat three dogs and four cats for some good friends. I sulked all week. They all slept on the patio, and were really no trouble at all to me, but I was so relieved when they left.

I realized that it was Christina's loving heart that made it possible for me to live with her, and to have my whole life changed, so how could I complain? In fact, I loved her so much that that was the problem. I didn't like to share. So I did have sympathy with Raphael, even though I was also jealous of him.

Christina had not been jealous of Rovero, I think. She was always willing to share with me. Why could I not always share with her?

Raphael began to talk to me again. "I think Christina is mad at me. The way I acted on the beach. But she should have told me she was going to Acapulco. It's my hometown!" He made no comment about his hometown girlfriend, but that I guess is a different matter in Acapulco.

He scratched my head between sentences. I assumed he'd brought the flowers for Christina. She hadn't complained to me, but Raphael, it seemed, felt guilty.

And suddenly, there she was, Christina, getting off the bus. It was always such excitement to see her. We both ran over to greet her. The flowers

were a good idea. At least, they served as a
conversation starter. And I tried very hard not to be
jealous of Raphael, even when he stayed for supper.

Chapter 14. Campus and a Car

I, Mancha, had not forgotten Rovero. A little scar tissue had formed over my grief. Just as with my mother, I found that, hard as it is, one must get on with it, take part in the daily process of living. So I played gently with Negrito, who thought of me as her mother. One moment she would tease and jump at me, the next moment cuddle up to me and purr. The two of us pretended to ignore the chicken, who often clucked at us as if she were scolding.

It was not long after our vacation that Christina took me with her in a taxi to a Used Car Lot. Now I'm sure most cars are used, some time or other. Such a waste if they weren't.

A Used Car Lot looks much like a parking lot, only one man owns all the cars. The man begged Christina to drive one car after the other, which she did. I was pleasantly surprised to learn that she could drive. It looked to me as if the man wanted to give her a car, but she didn't want to take one. I didn't interfere.

Several days later, Christina came home from school driving a shiny red van, which she explained to me was secondhand. Someone going "back to the States," had sold it to her. There were no hands in sight that I could see, but the car had plenty of seats to sleep on. *Dios!* What a home on wheels.

Little did I know the great changes this van would bring to Christina and to me. Because of this great automobile, I, Mancha, began to regularly attend the great University of Mexico, and Christina no longer rode the *autobus*, where she had twice lost her wallet to pick-pockets.

Losing a wallet in Mexico is a serious matter when you are not *Mexicano*. Not just the loss of the *pesos*, but the legal papers, which must be replaced with a great amount of waiting in lines and sometimes a trip to the border. So it was with great convenience for Christina and with great pride for me, to have a shiny red van to travel in.

It is not every dog that gets to attend a great center of learning like the University of Mexico, which, according to my restaurant owner friend, was in operation before the pilgrims landed on Plymouth Rock, which is on the eastern coast of the U.S.of A. My restaurant owner friend did not only know about revolutions; he knew geography of the whole world as well as history, because he had worked on a freighter in his youth.

I was teased a lot in my role as college student. Christina's friends kept asking if I'd become a veterinarian also. And would the *Universitaria* let me graduate without taking the exams, and how could I learn anything if I didn't learn to write first? They obviously hadn't heard of ears. I, Mancha, ignored them all. I already knew much more than they did about Mexico City, and about Christina. Education can take many forms, I have learned.

Most of Christina's classes were on the main floor and I could sit on the grass and look in on her. Other times I, Mancha, could actually attend labs with her, out at the barns and at the University Clinic, if I kept quiet, and out of the way. I listened and watched with great concern.

"You better keep your dog tags in plain sight, Mancha," one friendly doctor said, "or you'll end up in the experimental lab."

"You wouldn't dare," Christina said. "If Mancha ever disappears, you'll be held personally responsible."

The doctor may have been worried, but I wasn't! I, Mancha, was not going to disappear, least of all from sight of Christina.

I was not as nervous about losing her since we had the van, because now I could go everywhere with her. I loved the importance of sitting in the Doctor's office in the clinic. And I was so proud to sit beside Chistina in the front seat of the van.

I must admit I led a more sedentary life than when I roamed the streets with Rovero. I was gaining weight and feeling a bit lethargic from inactivity. But one can't remain an adolescent forever. Duty was becoming more important to me.

Christina's friends complained that I was acting more and more hostile towards them. I wasn't, really. I simply felt the need to protect her from everybody.

Christina laughed and said what I needed was another dog in my life. I thought she was very silly indeed. How could anyone replace Rovero?

Chapter 15. Chico

It came to pass that one night a young dog was abandoned at the front door of the clinic. He wore no tags, and was suffering from a broken hip and several bad bruises. Procedure would be to put him to sleep, but Christina was on duty.

"This is such a healthy-looking young dog except for his injuries," she said, and begged to operate on him and take him home to convalesce.

"With thousands of dogs in this world, you want this one?" the doctor in charge asked.

"I'll pay for the hip pin," Christine bargained.

X-rays were taken, and the operation went well. The next night we brought the patient home. He smelled of operating-room spray.

"Let's call him *Chico*," Chistina said. My first reaction was like the doctor's at the clinic. Why this one?

Chico looked as if his mother had been an eggbeater. Bits of longish hair stuck out here and there on his short coat, which was the color of mud. He had a tiny stump of a tail, and of course the hip area on one side was shaved and swollen, and stained with iodine.

He seemed to be a cross between Chihuahua and dwarf Airdale, if there is such a thing. I could not tell from the looks of Chico that we would become so attached to him.

That Chico! He wagged himself across the marble floor to me, slipping and sliding all the way, a silly grin on his face. If Christina had not already named him Chico, I would have named him Smiley. He slid into my front paws and bumped his sore hip. He yipped for a moment or two, but didn't stop smiling or wagging. Negrito and the chicken were spellbound.

That Chico always set a good example. Such good spirits. Later, when he found that the marble stairs were too steep and slippery for him to go down under control, did that stop Chico? No. He'd take a straight shot to the landing, pick himself up and go for the next section. Christina and I would almost have heart attacks, watching.

Of course Christina did not let him try the stairs until she had removed the metal pin and the wound had healed. Then when she saw how he managed the stairway, she said "Chico, at this rate you'll be back on the operating table shortly."

But she was wrong. Not for a long time did Chico have to return to the hospital, and then it was for a far more serious thing than a broken hip. I will

tell you about that later. Now, nothing bothered
Chico. As they say, his lucky star was on high.

I don't know if he'd had a home, before ours. It
would seem so, because he was what Christina
calls housebroken and minded her orders, and not
once did he attack the kitten, who was fast
becoming very close to a cat.

Chico was so smart. He could jump higher
than I could. That is, after his hip healed. He could
dance and do tricks. Later, I taught him to triumph
over the traffic and I loved to show him off to all my
many friends, when I wasn't at school.

Sad to say, Chico never attended the
University which would have been much better for
him than wandering the streets alone, and would
have maybe kept him out of trouble. At the moment,
however, he was recovering on the patio, and I,
Mancha, kept him company and got fatter with
idleness.

Chapter 16. Pregnancy & Puppies

One evening at the clinic, some time later, Dr. Rodrigez looked at me thoughtfully and said to Christina "I think it's too late to spay Mancha. If you ask me, Mancha looks pregnant."

"No, I don't think so," Christina said, also looking at me. "She's just putting on weight. She's too young. Never been in heat. I've been watching her closely."

"Hm," said he. "Then me thinks a miracle is being wrought."

Dr. Rodrigez wheedled me up on the examining table and without asking me anything, confirmed his suspicions.

"You are obviously right," Christina said, patting me gently on the abdomen. "I can't believe it."

I couldn't believe it either. I had put having puppies out of my mind as an experience not meant for me after Rovero so suddenly left my life without warning. Now to find I was well on the road to delivery, was shocking and confusing, and a little satisfying. This explained the changes in my body, the extra weight, the movement that I felt inside me.

After Christina got over her surprise, and the worry about what to do with the pups, she spoiled me rotten. Vitamin pills, whole milk, fresh beef and eggs three times a week, and boiled C-H-I-C-K-E-N. (She always spelled it out so our chicken wouldn't know!) The blessed event finally occurred and on the weekend, so Christina attended me at home. Negrito and the chicken slept right through.

Having never experienced birth before, except my own, everything seemed a little scary and painful, and I was glad Christina was there, although my natural instinct was to crawl into the darkest place I could find and suffer alone.

Christina wanted to observe the whole process in case anything went wrong, since I was so young. She allowed me to climb up on her bed and lie on an old blanket.

In the middle of the night, four slippery, wet, blind pups pushed through my birth canal. All squirming but one, who was stillborn. I licked it clean and nudged it time and again, but Christina finally took it away from me.

The second and third puppies were shiny black miniatures of Rovero, and the fourth one, smaller than the others, bow-legged and mud-colored, was a clone of my long lost mother.

I, Mancha, became brave only after it was all over. Then I had such thoughts as, why all the fuss, what could have gone wrong? It was nature's way and once a puppy starts to be born, there's no stopping it.

I did act excessively proud of my achievement, reproducing a Rovero and a match to my old mother. Not the same. And why pride? All I had done was to love and to mate with my now lost Rovero. Nature, and Doctor Christina, had done the rest. I was pleased that Christina let us all stay on her bed that night.

Sentiment aside, I was not an especially good mother. Negrito and the chicken had more natural instinct than I. Negrito wouldn't leave them for a minute, and the chicken fussed and worried over them like the broody hen she wanted to be. She sat on them as if they were baby chicks. They loved her warm feathers, and they loved her. They followed her around as if she were their blood mother. The only time they came to me, or I came to them, was meal-time. Chico adored those pups but he had not the milk to feed them.

"Mancha, tend to your puppies." Christina brought me up short as she sat down on the floor with them. "They're hungry, poor little things." She petted, and cooed, and made me very jealous. Miffed as I was, I lay down and nursed them.

Feeding them did make me feel important and rather maternal for the moment. They certainly enjoyed pulling at my nipples like little leeches, all three at once.

Christina kept saying how adorable they were, and chided me for my seeming coldness. I know, all babies are adorable, and I did love them, in my way, I suppose. But I was young, not mature enough to be a good mother.

I was caught up in the great world of the University and in spite of motherhood, I felt an even stronger pull to keep contact with that world, to continue my education, and to look after my mistress, whom I loved more than life itself.

Christina always seemed to give those puppies more attention to compensate for my shortcomings, so I, Mancha, suffered more than a few pangs of jealousy, but as always, everything finally worked out.

Chapter 17. The Landlord & Chico

When the landlord came to collect the rent and saw Christina's menagerie, he was quite upset. "Señorita, this is impossible. The chicken, I understand. The cat, it kills the mice. Even one dog, this Mancha, I can accept. Two dogs? No! No! No! And then you add three puppies?" The landlord drew himself up to his full height, which was about five inches shorter than Christina. "You must rid this apartment of the three puppies and one dog, or else move. Take your pick."

He spoke very forcefully, even though Christina was paying him in American dollars. I felt a low growl forming in my throat, but Chico, our darling Chico, smiled and danced before the landlord, turning full circle on his hind legs, begging for the landlord's approval. Chico's healed hip proved no disadvantage.

The landlord was so charmed by Chico that he made an offer to buy our lovable friend. When he found that Christina did not wish to sell Chico, he raised the rent five dollars, but did agree to let Christina keep the puppies until they were old enough to give away, and to let Christina keep

Chico until she graduated and went home to the states.

Both the landlord and Christina agreed that if Chico stayed in Mexico, Chico would make his home with the landlord. As always, my future seemed too vague and unpredictable to bother with. I, Mancha, would only worry about Christina, day by day. Everything else would take care of itself, I hoped.

A lot of things were happening at the University. Graduation parties. Picture taking. I was included in one large picture as the mascot of the Veterinarian class, and Dr. Rodrigez gave me an engraved medal with my name on it, an honorary degree from the Veterinarian school of that great University of Mexico. It was hard not to let all this glory go to my head when referred to by Christina's friends as Doctor Mancha. I was already such a cocky braggart to my old friends.

One sadness came upon me when my puppies were given away to friends of Christina's. I had thought I was immune to that kind of loss but when they actually were taken away, one by one, I realized they meant more to me than I had demonstrated. They were a last link to my youth and to Rovero.

Besides, they had become so entertaining to watch as they played together. If it hadn't been for

the attention of my good friends Chico and Negrito
and the chicken, I would have suffered even more
from the pups' absence.

The chicken suffered more than any of us. She
actually had a nervous breakdown and didn't lay
eggs for two weeks.

About the time we were all back to normal, Dr.
Christina performed her first operation under her
new title, and on me, Dr. Mancha. Dr. Rodrigez
assisted.

I awakened spayed, having missed the whole
performance, and feeling terrible with a sore
abdomen and plenty of hurt feelings.

"*Pobrecita*," Christina crooned, which means in
Spanish something like "Poor baby," and took me
home in our van, carried me up the five flights of
stairs and placed me on a soft pillow in the living
room.

I tried to sulk all afternoon, but Christina fed
me fresh ground meat, oatmeal and milk, some dog
food that I'm finally getting used to, and played her
guitar and sang American songs to me. It was
becoming more and more difficult to remain upset at
Christina.

That night, after Christina went to sleep, I
sneaked into her bedroom and crawled under her
bed, carefully avoiding her water glass. Marble floors

feel no worse than concrete sidewalks. Negrito and Chico joined me.

I allowed myself several soft moans for the pain I was feeling, but I, Mancha, had forgiven my *amiga* her trespasses, even though she didn't know it yet.

I took my time getting better. Chico amused me with his silly antics, and so did Negrito. And the chicken kept climbing all over me while I lay on the patio. Christina kept apologizing and explaining, for days, but there was no need. I would forgive Christina anything. And believe me, the time was coming when I would have to.

Chapter 18. Tragedy Strikes Again

I blame myself. If I, Mancha, had not dragged out my healing, I think I would have accompanied Chico on his walks about town and I would have kept him from touching the meat that had been set out for God knows what reason, laced with rat poison in a vacant lot.

Chico came home and was waiting at the door for Christina, so weak he could not stand. She knew immediately something was dreadfully wrong, but the damage was done. The terrible poison had begun its lethal work.

In spite of Christina's and three other veterinarians' work around the clock, including I.V.'s and I.M.'s and shots of adrenaline, it was to no avail. Within two days our beloved Chico passed from this world with his smile still on his face. His grief-stricken friends surrounded him. I could only howl.

Christina, forgetting her professional demeanor, cried. To have lost one of her very first official patients and he such a good friend, was a hard

thing for her to bear. I licked her hands and face
with feeling, at the same time also mourning for
Chico who would never dance again, or humor our
landlord.

Chapter 19. To the New World

Christina now began making plans to leave Mexico. She knew I would go anywhere with her. To school, to the beach, to *le banco,* even to the U.S. of A. I could scarcely recall what life was like before Christina. She had become my life. She couldn't leave me here alone in Mexico City. And she didn't plan to.

She gave Negrito and the chicken to Mrs. Gomez with the promise that never never never would Mrs. Gomez eat the chicken!

One day, Christina brought home a big white box with one end open. She put my favorite rug in there and coaxed me to go inside. "Nice Mancha," she said. I didn't stay in there very long, but she seemed pleased, anyway. Such simple things pleased my mistress in those days. Little did I know what was coming.

Several days later, some men came to our apartment and took all our belongings. It seemed to me they were thieves, but Christina would not allow me to bark at them. They took our furniture, Christina's clothes, the dishes, everything.

I growled through my teeth in spite of Christina. She said, "No! No!" and scratched my back. I shall never completely understand my mistress.

Finally, the apartment was bare except for two large canvas bags and the big white box with my favorite rug. Raphael arrived and helped carry bags and box out to the red van which he drove to the *Aeroporto* with the usual shouting and traffic jamming. Raphael kept saying we had plenty of time and not to worry, and Christina kept looking at her watch and moaning. We made it just in time to run in with the baggage and wave a quick goodbye to Raphael.

Christina put the big box down on the floor and

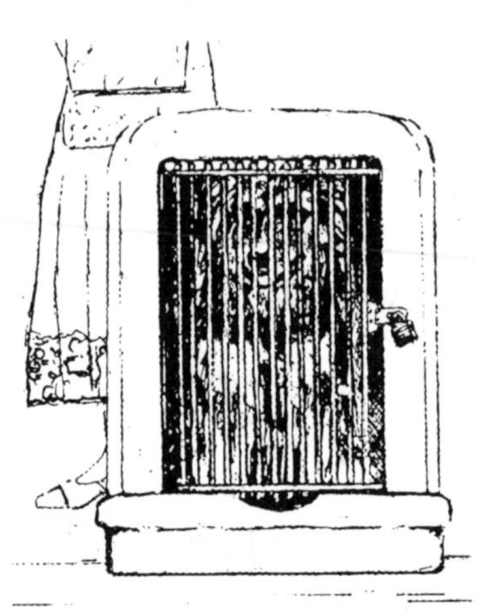

asked me to climb in. I didn't want to humor her with silly games in front of the people around us, but she slipped something into my mouth and stroked my throat until I swallowed it, then backed me into the box anyway.

She placed a grille on the open side, making a cage; and there I was, imprisoned by my own mistress. I whined, but she did not let me out.

The owners of two pair of blue covered legs obviously lifted the box and carried it away, somewhere, with me in it. I felt scared and upset, and very very sleepy.

Evidently I took a long nap. When I awakened there to my surprise was Christina. Nothing had happened to her, and she was letting me out of this box-turned-cage.

People were rushing about and I thought we were still at the airport terminal in Mexico City, but Christina said "Mancha, welcome to U.S.A. This is Los Angeles."

I swear I would have thought most of these *Angelinos* were *Mexicanos.* They looked like us, and talked like us.

Can you believe that after Christina took me for a long walk, on which we saw palm trees and friendly squirrels, we went through the same silly game all over again? The white box on the floor, the sticking something in my mouth, the backing me into that box, locking me in, two sets of legs lifting the box up with me whimpering and trying to stand.

This time Christina called "good girl, Mancha. See you in Boise."

Boise! Was Boise in the U.S.A. also? I fell asleep wondering.

Chapter 20. America. Idaho.

I was still groggy when I heard my mistress greeting me. She unlocked the box. I felt shy and strange this time. Fewer people were walking around in this Boise airport and they did not look like *Mexicanos*. They did not talk like *Mexicanos*. I pushed close to Christina.

"Come on, Mancha. Don't be afraid. The worst is over," she said, putting my leash on me. Easy for her to say.

Just then some strange man came up to her and greeted her joyously. Christina did the same to him. He seemed safe enough, so I relaxed a bit.

After we found our bags, the man and Christina carried them to a truck. A very nice truck. I was invited to sit in the front seat with them. I accepted.

The man, who's name was Jay, had a nice outdoor smell and I could tell he liked dogs. He drove for a long time into the mountains.

Christina got out of the car twice to run with me. That made me feel much better. Lots of space and fresh air like in the mountains of Mexico. I realized that if this was also the U.S. of A., I was going to like it very much, even without palm trees and *Angelinos* that look like *Mexicanos*.

After a while, although the time passed quickly with me watching the landscape and only half listening to the two of them talking of the University and of sheep, Christina said "This is it, Mancha. This is the ranch."

We drew up to a house, and got out. We were greeted by five other dogs. I had the feeling that they were all my second cousins.

"Her blood shows," Jay said.

Christina said "We'll see when she meets the sheep."

That evening, all the dogs were fed together, including me. It was worse than at the dog-pound. I've never seen such hungry dogs. By the time I'd worked my way to the food, it was all gone. Christina took care of that, however. She fed me later, by myself. I had the feeling that I, Mancha, was really going to like this ranch-life.

Chapter 21. Another Goodbye

The next morning, Christina had me climb in the back of the truck with three of the other dogs, who were really quite friendly in a reserved sort of way, as if they had more important things on their minds than passing the time of day with a stranger, but wanted me, the stranger, to feel at ease.

I didn't have time to dwell on how I felt about that, because we rode again through mountains, reminding me of the road to Acapulco. Then suddenly the truck stopped, tossing us off our feet. *Dios Mio*, I thought for a moment I was back in a Mexico City taxi. But the sounds of this traffic were different.

Hundreds of sheep were blocking the road. They looked just like the sheep I had seen at the *Zocalo*, but these were not in pens or staked. They were bleating and jumping and running free, and milling about. There were men shouting and dogs barking and running around nipping at the heels of the sheep. They were playing some kind of game far better than fetch and carry.

Christina put a leash on me, and good thing, because I, Mancha, was so excited I was trembling. I might have done foolish things if she hadn't held me. I might have jumped right into the middle of those sheep, or chased one of those frisky lambs, just the way I did on the road to Acapulco.

I felt sure I could do something important with these sheep if someone would only teach me what to do. These trained dogs worked and followed signals. Wouldn't it be possible for me to learn this also? After all, I had a degree from the great University of Mexico.

For the first time in my life I found it a great handicap not to be able to speak out in English or Spanish to Christina the way Jay or Raphael could. I tried Body language. I jumped and wheeled. I groveled at her feet. I pawed her. I wagged and wheeled in a crazy fit.

Christina understood more than I knew. Dios. Too much. She had Jay introduce me to Manuel, the Peruvian herder. He looked into my face carefully, and nodded. Felt my body, and nodded. "*Bueno.*

Bueno." He called in his lead dog, Blackie, and introduced me to him.

Christina took off my leash and I was suddenly shaken with another feeling. Christina was especially sober. Did she not feel my excitement? What did she want me to do?

"Mancha is a city dog," she said, petting me. "She knows nothing of rattlesnakes, and coyotes, or sheep."

"I'll fix that," Manuel said, showing his teeth.

Christina knelt then and hugged me tightly. "Mancha, Mancha," she said. "I'm going to miss you so much, but you must stay here with Manuel and be a good dog and learn how to tend sheep." Her voice broke and I knew she wanted to cry. But why should she miss me? I was right here in her arms.

"You stay here. I have to go to Chicago. Not for long."

What is Chicago? And how could she go without me, Mancha? I would go anywhere with her. She hugged me again, and I licked the tears rolling down her cheeks.

"You must stay with Manuel." I couldn't believe she meant it. "Stay!" Christina meant it. She said it so sharply that I sat right down again. *Dios Mio.* She was going to leave me. In this strange country. Alone. How could she desert me? I, Mancha would do anything for her. I looked at her, begging her not to leave me, begging in every way I knew how.

"I'll come back, Mancha. Next spring."

Next spring? How long was that? Sometimes three hours is too long. So is forever. She really was leaving me here with this strange herder who thank goodness spoke Spanish. I wanted to be with these sheep but not at the sacrifice of giving up Christina. Couldn't she understand that? I wanted always to be with her and watch over her. What would happen in Chicago without me to stand guard over her?

I tried to make her understand all this, but she ignored me. She turned away and climbed into the truck. "Let's go before I change my mind," she said. Jay started the engine and drove her down the mountain. She didn't look back. Not once.

I twitched and trembled as the truck disappeared. My heart felt scalded with bitterness. My Christina gone. My beloved Christina had left me. My heart beat Christina, Christina, Christina. I, Mancha, whimpered shamelessly.

"Come . . ." Manuel said, touching me with the toe of his boot. "We have work to do. Follow Blackie, and learn to be a good sheep dog." He patted me roughly on the shoulder then, and told me the *señorita* would return *mañana.*

Mañana might never come. My head sunk lower. I remembered that my mother had not returned. Rovero had not returned. The pups and Chico had not returned. Why would Christina return?

I had no choice but to wait and mind Manuel. Oh, Christina, you are breaking my heart!

"Mancha!" My name was called in a stern, deep voice. It was hard to lift my head, but even in my great sadness I felt that this herding sheep might be far more than a new game to play. It might prove to be my life's work.

I had spent much time at the great University of Mexico learning many things, and here, on this mountain with Manuel and Blackie, there was much more for me to learn.

With Christina's word "Stay!" still ringing in my ears, I stopped snivelling, and trotted after my new master to learn to be the best sheep dog in Idaho. I knew, even with a broken heart, that I, Mancha, could do it.

Chapter 22. Ranch Life Without Christina

The sun was shining on the Sawtooth Mountains, and the dust rose as the herd of sheep moved across the road and up the hillside. I, Mancha, tried to keep up with the sheepherder Manuel's best dog, Blackie. He seemed to be watching Manuel continually, and knowing arm signals that I could not know yet. That split second between Blackie's knowing an order and my trying to figure out just what Blackie was going to do, put me always way behind him, try as I would to keep up.

A new career is no easy task, no matter how willing one is to learn. There is so much one must know and so many strange things to do and see. Herding sheep is no simple matter, at best, I found out. My education at the great University of Mexico did not help me in the least.

"Don't crowd them!" Manuel shouted. Blackie barked at me to back off. It may have seemed like a game to me, when I first arrived with Christina, simply watching the dogs work the sheep. Now, I realized how serious a job it was. Blackie had his ears cocked always for voice signals from Manuel, who also waved his arms to signal. A whistle meant "Look at me," or "Stop and listen," or all three.

The excitement of seeing this big herd handled by one herder and a few dogs and having my chance to take part in the operation, was almost more than I could stand. I was sure I would die either of thirst or of a heart attack.

The steep slopes were apparently nothing to Blackie, but that first afternoon I was panting from the heat, and trying desperately to get more oxygen from the thin air to my lungs. I was not used to continuing an activity when tired.

Before the day was out, it seemed as if we'd run a hundred miles, back and forth, up and down at break-neck speed to cut off a wandering ewe or to pick up a straying lamb. My paws were torn and bleeding from the sharp rocks, but the excitement kept me from knowing that until we stopped at suppertime. I was too exhausted to eat much, but I kept coming back for water.

A good sheep dog does not run the sheep if he can help it. He runs himself, to keep the herd moving slowly in the right direction and to keep the herd together. He has to be alert to stragglers and alert to his herder's wishes; and alert to coyotes, cougars, rattlesnakes and bears.

Ordinarily a lone coyote will not fight a dog, but he can slip around the herd downwind, and nab a lamb or two. Sometimes coyotes kill for fun, and after their night's fun, a half a dozen young lambs lie dead, killed but not eaten. In any case, coyotes are not friends of the sheep dogs. I had not learned all this yet, as this was my first day on the job. As Manuel says, one learns from the experience.

That evening, after supper, when the sheep seemed to be bedding down for the night, Manuel brought out his guitar to sing his lonely heart out to the dogs, the sheep, and the full moon. All Spanish love songs. The darkness had lifted and the silvery light made great shadows on the grass. I could not keep my eyes open and fell asleep to the songs of the homesick Basque. *Sympatico.* If I hadn't been so tired I would have grieved a bit longer for my mistress Christina.

I don't know how much later it was when I was awakened by a low growl. Blackie was standing, ears up, staring at something coming up the hillside. A huge lumbering animal of some kind, half as big as a horse, and silvery bronze. Certainly not a sheep, I thought. Was this the coyote I had heard so much about?

Blackie gave three sharp barks to alert Manuel, and took off at full speed towards the advancing enemy. Within seconds, Manuel had jumped out of his blanket and dived for his rifle.

I was anxious to do the right thing, and it seemed to me this animal might be a robber or a molester of sheep. So I forced my aching body to get up and follow Blackie. I quit limping after the first few steps, caught up in the excitement of the chase.

I had never smelled or seen a bear before, and fear mixed half and half with the excitement as I got nearer. A bear, with one swat of his clawed paw, can send any dog clear to the big dipper.

Blackie obviously had no fear, or maybe his training overcame all other emotions. He never slowed down, but kept going right at the intruder.

The more scared I became, the harder I barked. I think that old bear must have thought an army of dogs were after him. He backed off, turned and lumbered off again.

Something else I had never heard. A gun shot! Manuel had aimed and fired. I was deafened by the sound for an instant, and as scared as if I'd been hit by the bullet. I yipped and cried for several moments. Then realizing how foolish I was acting, and that I was not hurt, I trotted back to camp with Blackie.

Manuel had missed his target. "I'll get him next time," he promised as he readied his gun. "You dogs did too good a job." He patted us hard so we knew that was a compliment.

In spite of the full moon and the excitement, I went back to sleep quickly and never moved again until just before dawn, when the sheep began to stir.

Blackie was already waiting instructions from our herder, but at that moment, I was torn between wanting to keep up with Blackie or hiding behind a rock and licking my sore paws. I decided that the only way that I, Mancha, could become the best sheep dog in Idaho was to stick with Blackie and learn everything I could. And so it went.

Chapter 23. School of Hard Knocks

I had a long way to go to become as good as Blackie. When he was on duty there was nothing that could distract him. He could work from dawn to dark without slowing down, without whining. He was also a first-rate teacher. While we were doing a chore he would approve or disapprove on the spot.

I was following on his heels one day, not paying attention to the ground, but only trying to keep up, when I learned another hard lesson: Don't follow anyone blindly.

Blackie suddenly sidestepped and I went tail over chin when I caught a leg in a groundhog hole. No bones broken, but from that moment on, I looked where I was going.

Blackie also taught me about rattlesnakes. They are like the taxis in Mexico City. If you are on foot, you stay out of their way. And that's tricky to do when there are so many. One of my first days sheepherding, I flopped myself down beside a big rock and idly watched this cute thing wigging and wagging on the rock's flat top. Suddenly Blackie was barking, pushing me aside. I heard a sound like a *maraca* band. The cute thing was a rattlesnake, now coiled and sending her warning before she struck.

Thanks to Blackie, the snake harmlessly swiveled off, leaving Blackie and me unharmed.

My lessons continued, over and over. I became stronger, with larger shoulders, bigger lungs. My paws became calloused and tough, so tough that cactus needles didn't penetrate.

One morning I found out why my coat was getting fuller and heavier. When we awakened, well before day-break, I saw that Blackie had turned all white. The ground was white. My first view of snow. The sheep had turned invisible. My nose felt cold when I touched the snow, and so did my paws.

"Too early for this," Manuel growled. He set about breaking camp and instructed us dogs to guide the sheep down the canyon. I was sad to leave the mountains where we'd spent so much time, and where I had learned so much.

After a long day of going downhill, we came to a nice little valley with a road and corrals. Trucks were waiting for us. We herded the sheep into the corrals, and the truck drivers and Manuel pushed the lambs into the trucks, separating the ewes.

I felt upset that they were taking part of our herd, but Blackie wasn't troubled at all. He was looking forward to the rest that comes to sheepdogs over the winter. Jay came over and talked to Manuel and patted me hard on the sides. "Christine will be proud of you, Mancha," he said. "We'll put a little fat on you by spring."

Christina! I looked at him with my heart in my eyes, and wagged my tail hard. He had no smell of her on him. She must be in Chicago forever.

Blackie came up to me then. He wanted to play. His duties were over for now. It finally dawned on me that so were mine. We chased each other's tail. We bit each other, growled, and made as if we were enemies. It was all for fun. Our working season was over.

Winter in Idaho is much different than in Mexico City. Colder. What is rain in Mexico is snow in Idaho.

Not just a thin blanket of snow like we had as a warning in the mountains, but lots and lots of snow. Snow that comes up to the rooftops in drifts when the wind blows. Snow so deep that it causes dogs and people lots of trouble when they try to walk in it.

When the sun crusts the snow, then one can walk on top. Those days, Blackie and I would hunt jack rabbits. It didn't matter if we caught one or not. We had fun chasing them.

Jay kept paths open from the house to the sheep sheds and to the barns, so there was plenty of walking to do. Blackie and I liked to hang around the sheds, checking the ewes. Sometimes, Manuel would invite us into his bunk house, and sing his folk songs for us. I would get a little uncomfortable in the heat with my heavy coat, but I tried not to show it for his sake. He was always homesick and needed company.

Winter was also a good time for me to cuddle up next to Blackie and doze off with boredom, and dream of the good old days with my mistress Christina. Then I'd whimper, wondering if I would ever see her again.

Chapter 24. Return of Spring

November, December, January. Those are the deep days of winter in Idaho. Sheep ranches start coming to life again in late February. Early lambs start being born. Early March, the herds are being formed, horses picked and dogs chosen, for herding on the desert. The excitement is almost unbearable for a sheep dog, because he knows he's going back to work again. I, Mancha, was no exception.

The lambs are so precious, and smaller than we are. Of course young lambs make herding that much harder. Not only to keep track of them, but to protect them from freezing to death or from being eaten by coyotes or some other enemy. An eagle can manage to lift up a very young lamb and fly with him up to his mountaintop nest.

At the start of the season, the old ewes are well behaved, but some of those young mothers can't get it in their heads to stick with the group for protection.

As Manuel checked out dogs and horses, he divided Blackie and me. "Mancha can be head dog for the other herder." Can you imagine my pride? I, Mancha, a boss dog! Yet at the same time, I knew I was going to miss Blackie. I was also a little nervous. What if I made some big mistakes and Blackie wouldn't be there to cover for me? What if I lost my lambs to the coyotes? Or split the herd? And who was to be my herder? Would I like him as well as I did Manuel? Or would he like me?

Many of these questions were answered shortly. Jay drove up in his truck from somewhere, and out stepped, -- you won't believe this, I can't believe it yet,-- out stepped my mistress, Christina. Christina from the end of the world, Chicago. My owner. I did the worst No-No and jumped up on her. She this once allowed it, trying to hold me in her arms. All sixty pounds of me. She laughed and we fell together on the ground. I turned myself inside out with joy, as we busied ourselves, hugging and kissing. I licked the tears off her face.

I, Mancha, forgave her immediately for leaving me here alone, without her. How could I think of sulking? I had so much to share with her. I had learned so much. I, Mancha, had grown up.

And now, she was to be **my** herder. I was to be **her** top dog. This moment was the most glorious of my life. To think that she and I would be doing this herding of the sheep together, forever. Christina & Mancha, *Amigas* forever.

Afterword

The *Christina* of the story in I, MANCHA is
patterned after a young woman raised in a Chicago
suburb and who from the age of six wanted to be a
veterinarian. Neighbors would bring her birds injured
from confrontation with cats, dogs and picture windows.
She patiently nursed them until they could fly away on
their own, or until life departed from their bodies, as often
was the case, and she sadly buried them in the back yard.

When a teenager, her most signal success was
nursing seven baby rabbits to maturity after their mother
was destroyed by a neighbor's dog. Every two hours, day
and night for weeks, she hand-fed each tiny voracious
rabbit with a doll's baby bottle. Not one failure.

After graduating from college in biology and
spending a year studying micro-biology, she -- in order to
gain more experience to list on her applications for vet
schools -- found a job to help with lambing at the
Wrigley ranch in Idaho.

Her love of animals plus her willingness to help
with Caesareans as well as to shovel manure, impressed
her boss. When lambing was done, and he found himself
short a herder, he hired her to take one band of sheep:
over two thousand head -- in the high desert first, and
then in the mountains for summer, alone with two horses
and two dogs.

She was the first female sheepherder in the state,
and that year had the lowest number of lost lambs of any
of the herders at the Wrigley ranch as well as the best
weight gain for her lambs.

At a time when women were not encouraged to
enter veterinarian medicine, she found her niche in
Mexico City where she learned Spanish at the same time

she was learning veterinarian medicine. Five years are required to earn the vet degree there as compared to four in the United states, plus six months of working as a vet for the government in the hinterlands for allowing her, a foreigner, to attend the great University of Mexico.

She then had to intern a year in the U.S.A. and take our government's special exam for foreign graduates before she took the national and state boards here. She is now a practicing vet with her own clinic out of Burley, Idaho. She has two children who also like animals. They have a bird, a ferret, numerous cats and dogs, several lambs and goats.

Mancha, the heroine of the book and teller of the tale, is based on a real dog who was also wise, empathic, strong, brave and passionately loyal, one of the best sheep dogs in Idaho. Ole!

The cover art for I, MANCHA is a photographed portion of the original painting, "Sheep Camp in the Sawtooths" by Ralph Harris, conceived originally for the state poster celebrating Idaho's 100th anniversary.

A man of many talents, Ralph Harris knows the territory. Born and raised in Idaho, he is of Basque origins and has done his share of herding sheep. He is also a ski instructor during the winter season at the Sun Valley resort.

Ralph Harris has also received national recognition for his art work, which include his commissioned portraits of World War II generals, permanently displayed at the Wright-Patterson Air Force National Museum in Dayton, Ohio.

He lives permanently in the Valley area with his wife, Jacqui Harris, who is now manager of condominium operations at Sun Valley.

Illustrator for the text of I, MANCHA, David J. Rau, was raised in California. He attended the Laguna School of Art at Laguna Beach. He has a varied background as sculptor, make-up artist and set-designer. He was commissioned action sports portraits for the San Diego Padres, the L.A. Lakers and the L.A. Rams. The Olympic Fine Arts Committee commissioned him for a portrait of the Olympic Silver Medalist, Picabo Street, Idaho's own. I, MANCHA was David's first book illustration assignment.

David now resides in the Los Angeles area with his wife, Mary. David is a grandson of the late David Wallerstein, a former bi-annual guest and admirer of Sun Valley. The artist is just as enthusiastic about the area as his grandfather was: fishing and hiking in the summer, skiing and dining in the winter. He also has found creative time to remodel an old house and build a new one, which they use as their vacation home.

About the Author

Carol Spelius lives in Deerfield, Illinois. She has always loved dogs, cats, horses and people, not necessarily in that order. She has a great appetite for reading: Cereal boxes, catalogs, Shakespeare, four-year-old magazines, novels, autobiographies. She watches TV when too tired to read or write or when doing mindless things like wrapping packages or sorting papers.

Carol Spelius has a short-story collection, AQUEUS & OTHER TALES that won the Friends of Literature's Vicki Penziner Matson Award in 1991. She also has a poetry collection, GATHERINGS, released in December, 1995 and a collection of essays called HOW WE GOT HERE FROM THERE: One Family's Odyssey, in 2000, and and of course takes credit for I, MANCHA, in 2001.